i

QUANTUM MURDERS

THE BEGINNNING

Rajasekar Natarajan

Table of Contents

iii

Dedicated to all those who interacted with me !!!

Challenge

I am "D" – Dinesh working as a detective in Crime Branch of Investigation in the rank of Assistant Superintendent of Police (ASP). We are going to take the flight to US in next 14 hours. Infact for me this is going to be my first flight experience. Last few days I have a strong gut feeling that this travel is going to be a rollercoaster experience for me. My instinct says all I had believed in my life so far is going to be questioned?

Are you asking me why am I traveling to US then? I have a sister who is working in US. She loved a guy and they both got married 2 years ago. Eight months back she delivered a baby boy. Knowing this me and my mom could not control our excitement and we wanted to be with them spending time with baby. I see you are asking me why wait for eight months.

What to say being a government employee traveling to foreign nations is not so easy. Especially when you are in a central government job this will be a Himalayan task. To apply for a passport or a visa one must obtain No Objection Certificate from concerned departments keeping the superiors informed well ahead of time. If we screw up something in our job or disappoint the superiors this could easily take few years.

Even though If we manage to get necessary documents and approvals, I need to provide answers for questions like where am I traveling? Who am I going to meet? What is the purpose? Where am I going to stay there? How long? Who is sponsoring my trip?

In a way the process is there to make sure money, or an asset or travel is not offered as a bribe in exchange for favoring any person approaching them to go against the law. If you are in uniformed services or defense related research organization, it ends there. At any cost nation doesn't want to give an employee a chance for collaborating with anyone outside the country that can go against nations interest.

After 2 long years of wait I managed to get my passport, US visa and even more importantly 2 months of leave to travel.

"D have you packed all your things? Your sister told it is freezing there." this is my Mom Parvathi approaching me with the question.

After four long years she is going to see her daughter and the newborn in our family. As per airline ticket we are allowed to carry up to 60 Kg baggage. But my mom had booked additional 60 Kg and filled it with dress, toys, food items and other things that will be useful for the daughter and newborn. However, I stumbled upon a new, not new an old roadblock for this travel. I am very much thinking about that for the last few days.

Now Mom entered my room asking, "Did you informed the taxi guy to pick from home and drop us in airport."

Yes, Mom I did.

Looking at my thinking face, she asked "in which world are you?"

Nothing Mom, it is all about the Minister's daughter case. Deputy General of Police is putting pressure to solve this case before I leave.

Mom, I remember once you mentioned there are assistance service available in airports. will you be able to travel alone if I book the service for you? I will join you in another 3 or 4 days or else I can travel with you now, and I will comeback in a week once the function is over.

Mom is upset and she told, "Son - US is not in few hours reach. Just to reach there it will take a day for us. Better you talk to your sister, she is expecting both of us eagerly. Moreover, she has plans to conduct baby's tonsure function at Pittsburgh temple. Being an uncle, you must hold the baby on your lap during this function. Now if you go and tell her that you won't be there for it, she will be super upset. I know you have been working on that case for long time now. Are you going to get any clue in next few days which you haven't got for last six seven months? Better pass on the case to another personnel and travel with me. You can get back to this case if you want after we return."

Ok Mom, I will inform the superiors and make sure I will travel with you.

I can see you are asking me what is that case which is making my head spinning. Vidhya is a daughter of a big politician whose party is strong opponent to ruling party. Eight months back she got married to the son of a Minister from the ruling party. Within six weeks of her marriage, she was found dead mysteriously in her house. Parents being powerful and influential politicians, both the sides are giving pressure to the department to nab the criminal as soon as possible.

Enquiring some of Vidhya's friends we learnt she was in love with a boy before her marriage. He happened to be her colleague. Due to pressure from her parents and threat for her boyfriend's life eventually she agreed to marry the groom of their parents wish. After her death naturally the lover became our first suspect.

We brough in the forensic team and completely swept the place of murder. Except for the DNA specimen of husband and wife who lived in that house we could not get even a single clue. We decided to go for another round of search, this time we turned the house upside down. Due to the frustration, I kicked the mat near the main door. Something popped out from under the mat. It was a sealed envelope. Upon opening it we found a note saying, "you will receive a justice soon for cheating me". Our suspicion on her ex-boyfriend got confirmed.

We reached her company in Bangalore and enquired about the where abouts of her boyfriend on the day of murder. Office CCTV cameras, ID Card Turnstile swipes, HR data and meetings he had with his customers confirmed he wasn't away from Bangalore for at least last few days before and after that murder. More to this, soon he heard the demise of his girlfriend he went to the top of the building and was about to commit suicide. Luckily, we stopped him and informed his family about his condition. Meanwhile we asked his friends to watch over him before his parents can reach from their hometown. Office HR team had promised us to put him under counselling.

We investigated the husband too; our findings confirmed that he was also nowhere close to murder scene at the time of murder. He was in his party office organizing meetings for upcoming election campaign.

We were back to square one. The envelope did not carry neither a postage stamp nor any courier company's stamp. It seemed like an anonymous warning note dropped under the door but didn't get noticed by anyone from the home. The Handwriting also didn't match with anyone close to her.

All my instinct told was, this is the letter which is going to show who is the killer. It's been seven months now we could not get any solid leads.

From my childhood I was more inclined towards solving complex and puzzling things. My mom used to tell it is a gift I inherited from my father. I had it in my DNA to solve any challenges before me at any cost. To add fuel to the fire now there is enormous pressure from higher ups and their parents.

What mom said is right, what I could not solve for months now will I be able to solve in next 14 hours. Probably a change of picture from this travel might help me come back and solve it. I decided to call my superior to inform it.

When I was about to take my phone, very same second my phone rang. It was my sister coming in a video call.

Hey D, It's me.

Yes, Sister its 100th call in last 2 days.

All set for your travel?

"We are almost ready", I replied.

Have you bought and packed the medicines I asked for Bharath? (Bharath is my sister's husband.)

Yes, yes, I had already bought it and packed.

What's my nephew doing?

I just gave him a bath, going to put him to sleep.

Meanwhile over the video I saw him coo'ing and blowing raspberries.

I heard my sister telling her baby, look at you, blowing raspberry and spitting all over you. I must give you bath one more time.

Ok dude, I must go now and make him sleep. Just ring me before you are about to leave, saying it, she ended the call.

The scene of my nephew blowing raspberries and spitting bubbles over my sister something struck me. The anonymous letter we found inside the envelope; I was able to open it swiftly. The envelope was not sealed using an adhesive, why can't it be saliva a popular way of sealing letters when we don't find adhesive nearby.

Immediately I called to my colleague Kandan.

He picked the phone and asked me to go on bro.

I started saying not sure just a hunch, do you remember the letter we recovered in Vidya's case?

Yes bro.

Can you send the envelope we got along with the letter to Forensic team? Ask them to check did the murderer used saliva to seal the envelope? If it is so, can you ask them to run a fast DNA match with our list of suspects. If it matches with anyone, he must be the killer we are looking for.

Sure, bro I will do as told.

Exactly 5 hours before for my flight, I got a call from Kandan brother.

Brilliant Bro, from the fast DNA runs we identified the suspect. They found the saliva and the DNA matched with her Husband's. Detailed matching run is going on and we should get the report in another 36 hours. Should we wait for it?

Hearing him, I replied to myself I thought so. No, you don't have to wait. I will talk to SP - Superintendent of Police. Please bring him in custody for an enquiry. I will be in office in another 15 minutes, rest we will talk in person.

Informing my mom to be ready, I reached my office. Before I reached there Vidya's husband was brought in for enquiry. Knowing we got hold of him with evidence, he agreed to confess.

Having no other way, he started by saying I came to know of my wife's past affair through the party workers. They were mocking me behind my back. I felt ashamed and went to home immediately. Me and my wife had an argument over this, out of the emotion I pushed her aside and went inside a room and locked the door.

After some time when I came out, I saw her in a pool of blood. Seems when I pushed her, she fell and got hurt badly in the back of her head. I checked here pulse and breathing. She was already dead. Knowing I might face jail time, just to divert the attention I kept this letter and left the place as if nothing happened.

Why didn't the handwriting match?

I am ambidextrous, so I wrote this letter in my non-dominant hand.

Something didn't add up with the postmortem report.

When I had to sign in order to receive the body in Government Hospital after postmortem, I saw the same pad had the doctor's note on time of death and cause of death. I just changed the time of death from, 01:00 PM to 07:00 PM. Out of fatigue due to workload seems doctor signed the reports prepared by his office staff. You guys are very well aware of what happened after that.

SP came out of the enquiry room and greeted me saying genius D. You really cracked this case with your wit. There is going to be elections in next 3 months. The opposite party would make this political to get sympathy votes. Better you take a break from this. We will handle it from here. For some more time just be careful as the case involves heavy weight politicians.

Informing SP and Kandan bro I proceeded with my trip to America. I called my mom over phone and told her the **challenge** for our travel is no more there.

Travel

After crossing a usual traffic jam, I finally reached home. I saw the taxi had already arrived and loaded our baggage. I went into the house calling my mom's attention. I saw her with drops of tears in her eyes looking at the photograph of my father who died months before I was born.

On seeing me approaching her she asked, "**D** Shall we leave?"

I said yes and went into my room to grab my shoulder bag. Informing the neighbors to keep a watch over property and garden, we started towards the airport. On our way to airport, we were asked to take a diversion due to a small demonstration. Seeing the protest placards I sensed it is nothing, but the political game SP had mentioned. We crossed it with a smile and managed to reach Airport on time.

As soon as we entered the airport, the news of my case was all over the channels. Opposition party is trying to take advantage of this situation by tarnishing the image of the ruling party.

Since my mom had lived in US for a while in her later twenties she navigated me easily through check-in desk, immigration, customs, and security check. When we reached our boarding gate, we had exactly 45 minutes before our flight. As I could see the boarding hasn't started, I heard the announcements for our flight number DC6789 from Chennai to Pittsburgh USA one stop over via Dubai is delayed by an hour due to technical reasons.

I had a slight headache, felt like having a tea would help. I went to a restaurant inside the airport and handed over 20 INR asking for a Tea. He looked at me up and down and handed me over the menu card. A cup of tea was 140 INR. Shocked by the price I asked for a bottle of water, he said 100 INR. Chips he responded 80 INR, I dropped the 20 INR in the jar next to him saying keep it as tips and moved away from the place.

I quenched my thirst by drinking the water from drinking water fountain inside the airport. After refreshing myself I reached my gate. By that time, I saw the boarding had already started. Me and my mom got into the plane. After 4 hours of travel, we reached Dubai. Since the same plane will be taking us to US after an hour of stop over, we were asked to sit back. We took off again once the passengers from Dubai to US-Pittsburgh joined us.

After 18 hours of tiring and exhausting travel, we finally landed in US soil. My mom answered the questions asked by Immigration officer fluently in English who also verified our travel documents in parallel. After few minutes he handed over our documents back to us saying, "Welcome to America".

We collected our baggage coming out of the conveyor belt and placed it in a trolley. As we approached the airport exit doors, I saw my sister eagerly waiting for our arrival. On seeing us she ran to us and hugged me and mom with happy tears. I asked her where is my nephew?

She pointed towards a direction and responded "Look over there he is with his dad? I went to her husband Bharath and greeted him and took the baby in my arms. In next few minutes from my hands, he hopped on to his grandma and didn't come to us.

It took an hour and half from airport to reach home. We didn't notice it took us that much time because of the stories we shared on our way.

First week was full off rest. Later that week we had the tonsuring celebration as planned for my nephew. By that time, we had got over with our jet lags and our body clock started adopting to new time zone.

One fine morning my sister asked me why don't we go to Niagara Falls next week?

I asked her, Whether Bharath would get a week off?

She responded saying Yes, in fact he has an interview in New York and he is the one who suggested this plan.

Great, where are we going to stay there?

Bharath's family owns a home there in New York. Now his sister is staying there alone. We will join her for few days.

I replied with excitement, "I am looking forward to going out."

Then she turned to my Mom and asked her response.

Immersed in the middle of thoughts, mom responded with "Dear what did you ask?"

"I was asking about the New York trip mom."

Sure, sure we can go. Mom replied and went back into her thoughts.

In the middle of our discussion Bharath approached me asking "D - are you free today?"

"All-day Bharath".

You said it's been a while you had a good tea right.

Yes, yes. For the tea I got during my flight where they just gave hot water, tea bag, milk powder and sugar separately, I made myself one but could not drink it. It tasted so weird; you won't believe the tea I used to have in my office compound tastes far better.

When I reached here, I see most of you are drinking only coffee, that too black without sugar or milk. Sister told we will buy some tea powder when we go to Walmart next time.

Seeing me I am longing for a good tea, Bharath replied, there is an Indian restaurant near my university. Tea and Coffee taste awesome there. I have a small work in my university, if you are free, we can go there and have lunch.

Sure Bharath, let me know when we must start.

May be ten minutes from now.

Ok then, I will get ready and come.

Around eleven o clock we reached the university where Bharath is working. We parked the car and walked 500 meters from there. From the far, I saw a home converted into a restaurant. The parking was full. We just crisscrossed few vehicles in the parking and reached the entrance.

I saw ten to fifteen families were taking a buffet lunch. There were few students too.

As soon as we entered Bharath chatted with some random employees, they spent few minutes with him among their busy schedules.

Suddenly he made me wait in the table and went inside the kitchen and brought us a cup of tea.

Out of respect, I asked him why are you doing this? If we ask the waiter, he is going to bring it?

Bharat replied, "It's nothing Dinesh, I had worked in this restaurant as a parttime employee when I was doing my studies in this University. I know the nook and corners in the kitchen."

Moreover, its common in this country for students to take up a part-time employment. As they work and earn, they learn the value of hard-earned money. Some people use this money for their studies. Some see this as an opportunity to improve their social skills by learning to work or communicating with different people. Haven't you seen it in news even President Obama's daughter worked as a waiter few years back during a summer.

To me it was surprising, in India sending kids to a job before they graduate is seen as a status issue for parents, especially down south. Whereas here it is seen as an opportunity to experience real world and enhance their skills.

Bharat continued "During weekdays students and professors from this university father will be here for the taste of coffee, tea and breakfast served here. Especially if there is any popular sporting event there won't be a place to stand to watch it on TV over there. On the weekends Indian families in this town crowd here to taste the buffet food."

Talking to me he turned his head and asked an employee where John is?

"John and Mary sister went to New York to attend a spiritual discourse. They should be back tomorrow morning.", employee replied.

Oh, is it? Fine, can you let him know that I came here to meet him. Since I will be out of town for a week, I will meet him once I come back.

Yes, for sure, employee replied.

After having our lunch and tea, Bharath asked "Shall we leave to home?"

"What happened to the work you came for?" I asked.

I came here to see John, since he is not here, I will meet him later.

Are you planning to start a business taking his opinion?

Smilingly he replied "No I came here to discuss about my research"

Oh, Is it? Is he your supervisor?

No, No. John is an Indian who got settled in America when he was young. I remember him once saying, due to his family situations he had to drop out of his Science majors from the college. Even today he keeps him updated by reading science magazines, discussing with university students and professors coming here.

He is simply brilliant. Once during a science quiz show in TV, he impressed everyone by answering all the questions at ease while we were struggling. He can come up with a layman explanation of complex theories or concepts with his brilliance. He is a Sci-Fi movie addict too. If he would have continued his studies maybe he might have become one of a great physicist or a scientist in the world.

Infact when I was working here, he helped me complete my assignments by giving a different dimension to my work. He will not give out answers directly. Instead, he will ask me leading questions, the thinking process, or answers to which will open out the different perspective or brilliance in us.

I have asked him why are you doing this? You could have given the answers directly.

To which he replied, I don't want to give you a direct answer that would kill your creativity or thinking ability and make you dumb. Instead through questioning you, you challenge your understanding on this topic to get the answer as well I get different perspectives on the same topic based on ideas and answers from the discussion.

He is really a gem of a personality and a hard worker. Without his effort he wouldn't have made this small place a crowded restaurant.

He is the one who inspired me to select my research topic towards quantum computing. I got very old papers from an author named RV from a journal. Infact, I came here to discuss about those papers with him.

I think I am boring you talking about my work. By the Way, How do you like being in America? How is your work going on? I heard you solved a cold case recently. What are your plans for your marriage? We chatted on different topics as we reached home that evening.

Meetings

Next day morning after 4 hours of travel we reached the Niagara Falls as planned. Bharath's sister Mythili joined us there. After seeing the breath-taking view of the place, enjoying the boat ride that took us close to the waterfalls, aquarium, and nice food we reached home in New York in the middle of the night. Next two days we roamed all around New York's landmark places like Empire State building, Times Square, Wall Street, Brooklyn bridge, Twin tower site, Statue of Liberty.

Due to the interview plans for Bharat we decided to stay indoors and get enough rest for next 2 days.

However, next day morning I woke up from bed very early. Just after my usual morning routines I walked towards the living hall with a cup of tea. I saw my sister and mother sleeping next to the baby in a room.

Mythili and her friends started their work from living room at 0700 AM on their startup idea. An idea to create platform where one can share, exchange, or sell their preloved toys or books of or for their kids.

I saw Bharath was getting ready for interview. I casually asked him can I join with him.

He responded saying sure D. I can drop you near a landmark place if any on our way. You can tour the place and I can pick you up while returning from the interview.

We left from home around 0800 AM and keyed in the destination we wanted to reach on google maps. It showed it will take almost an hour and half to reach there.

As we crossed the city limits, Bharath asked me are you and mother-in-law not disappointed for getting married without informing you?

In thought in my mind "It is very painful to be not part of my own sister marriage". But I gave silence as my answer.

Understandingly he went ahead and apologized to me. He told months before the marriage I lost my parents in a road accident. I was supposed to drive them that day but due to work I asked them if they can drive on their own. Later in the day I got a call from police to come to a hospital where my parents were brought dead from an accident. Had I gone with the plan and given them a ride they would be alive with me now. This thought of mine took me into depression. It was your sister's friendship, care, love, and support that brought me out of depression. During those months the time I spent with her, I also learnt there is more than friendship between us. We both realized we loved each other crazily. The moment I realized I can't live without her for a second, I proposed her asking will you marry me. In next few days we got married in presence of few of our friends.

From the day you arrived, I could see from Aunt's face she is not happy for us getting married without her presence. Due to guilt, I am unable to face her.

I interrupted and said, Bharath honestly, mother and I had our disappointments. Not being able to present in an only daughter and only sister marriage was a real pain. We dreamt of her marriage. After your marriage, sister called us several times and convinced us. The second when we came to know your son was born all the worries flew away. Mom started going to temples and pray for your family's wellbeing. She had counted the days to come and visit you. You can stop worrying about this and be a normal person around her.

After few minutes of drive, thinking of changing the topic Bharath asked "What do you think about Mythili?"

I asked, "Who your sister?"

Yes.

She is a smart, intelligent, and independent women. I think all these qualities naturally runs in your gene.

Even with the heater on, it is getting cold inside the car, right? Bharath replied.

I understood he is meaning I am trying to flatter him.

Bharath went on and said I think she likes you.

What makes you say that?

I saw her looking and going around you in the Niagara Falls. Also, wherever we stopped to take photo, she preferred standing next to you. To confirm it, this morning, I saw the wallpaper in her phone it was a photo where you both stood as a couple.

Smilingly I said, it can't be like that. That is the first day I even **met** her. I think she might be seeing the photos taken on that day in her mobile and you got it wrong. Moreover, I am working with the police department. Even I don't know when I will be at home or when I will be on duty. I don't think my kind of lifestyle will suit her.

Bharat responded saying, Mythili is interested to get settled in India after her marriage. She doesn't like the fast-paced lifestyle here. This is the same reason she quit her high paying job and do what interests here.

If you like her and ready to take her hands in marriage, I will talk to Aunt. If you don't like her, it's ok, we will search for a suitable groom.

In my mind I know I had already fallen for Mythili. While I responded to him saying can I have a word with her and let you know my decision before I leave, he stepped on the brake all of a sudden.

When I looked outside, I saw a security had asked us to stop our vehicle.

On lowering the window, I heard him saying Welcome to Quantum Research Labs. May I know the reason for your visit.

Bharath answered to him as Interview and showed him the call letter he had in his phone.

He starred at me and asked, Sir and you.

Bharath replied, "He just accompanied me."

Security guard responded, "Sorry sir, Visitors are not allowed inside the campus. Pointing towards a direction, he mentioned he can wait in the cafeteria which is to your right?"

Bharath parked his vehicle and we both got out of the car. He asked me to wait in the cafeteria and walked around 200 meters to the main facility for his interview.

While I was waiting, I was having a tea and reading the magazine to kill the time. I got a weird feeling someone is watching over me.

The person from the cashier's desk approached me and asked me are you the son of RV?

I didn't answer him as I was thinking who this person in this foreign land is, asking me a question that too in my mother tongue.

He went on and said you resemble my friend Rajesh's wife Parvathy's face. That is why I asked you.

Coming to senses I said, "One minute you are right my mom's name is Parvathy and my father is Rajesh Vaidyalingam."

Yes, yes. When he worked with this lab, we used to call him RV.

What are you saying? Did my father work here?

He went ahead and asked how is my father, mother and sister doing?

I responded, "Don't you know my father died in an accident at work?"

He froze for a minute and said Yes, Yes. Then he narrated the incident happened on the day before my dad's death. He also shared some family photos from his phone and recollected the days of their friendship.

Finally, he sat with me to have lunch and invited my family to his home handing over the visiting card.

Call for duty

In the middle of our conversation, I got a call from my chief.

As, I answered his call, he quickly asked me, "D did you see the news?"

I said No and asked him anything important Sir?

Yes, Sadananda Guru a well-known spiritual leader from our country who was giving speech and answering Q&A with students in York University has been kidnapped.

What are you saying sir? He is a most celebrated person, right? I know he had declared that I am not a god or God man, and no one has to follow him. All he claims is "I am a same person as every other human being. The only superpower I obtained is through genuinely researching and finding how this body and mind works and what we can do to keep it healthier. I am just teaching those yoga techniques which worked on me to others for other's benefit."

Yes, you are right. Throughout the country his disciples and students are sad. TV channels are telecasting this news every other second. Even our state Chief Minister is his disciple. He personally called me over phone and asked me what we can do in this regard. Moreover, seems Prime Minister office and foreign secretary is pushing the US government to act fast on this matter and rescue him in 48 hours.

From our department they have asked us to collect details of members in our force who is presently in US. For now, you were the one staying close to the place of incident. We have few more officers who would join with you to form a search and rescue mission incase if we don't get enough traction on this matter from the US government.

I am cancelling your leave immediately and you are on duty from now on. First thing please visit the FBI office and collect the required details on this case and update me. I have asked the department to share with you the details of the person whom you need to meet with. Also, we will inform them of your visit.

Ok sir, just send me over the details. I will follow-up and update you the status.

After the call, while I was thinking what to do next, Bharath came and tapped on my back after his interview.

He said sorry for keeping me waiting and asked should we leave now?

"No problem we can leave.", I replied.

When I was about to enter the car, Mr. Singh came towards me running. Seeing Bharath inside the car, he handed over a leather bag secretly to me and said it belongs to your father.

On opening the bag, I found some receipts which were too old and erased over time. Few visiting cards, a Compact disk, spectacle, a pen, and a small bracelet. I thanked him and got into the car.

On the way back I just enquired Bharath, how did the interview go?

With lot of happiness he replied, once I defended my Ph.D. thesis, they asked me to come and join the next minute. Moreover, they offered to sponsor my research and patenting expenses completely. They were generous enough to offer me to use their computing facilities anytime.

It is the topic I took for my research that fetched me this role. They praised my efforts in this field a lot. Infact, they said it with full confidence it could be none other than me who could complete the job half done by a predecessor RV.

The moment he spelled the name RV, I felt a chilling sensation that started from by lower backbone and rose it to my head.

I thought of changing the topic and requested him to drop me in the FBI office citing the new case which on my way.

When we reached the FBI Office, I got down from the car and asked Bharath to leave. I approached the security with details who guided me to the reception staff for assistance. I told the staff that I am here to meet Asha Balachandran. She asked me to sit on the couch and informed Asha over the phone.

After 15 minutes of wait, Asha met me in the building reception. She took me to her office and started sharing details about Sadananda Guru's missing case.

I asked her how did he disappear?

While answering the students in the auditorium he collapsed and fell on the floor. From there he was taken in an Ambulance which went missing.

Heart attack? I asked.

No, Kidnapping.

How do you say it is Kidnapping?

When he was talking, over the microphone they released some sort of gas which made him uneasy and collapse. Looks like a well-executed case of kidnapping.

What about the Ambulance?

When enquired it seems the University ambulance which is expected to take him to hospital arrived late by 10 minutes. That is when they got the doubt and informed the police.

Also, we got reports stating the ambulance used for kidnaping was found abandoned near an old bridge. My team members are at the site.

Any Individual or organization came forward claiming responsibility for this kidnapping?

No.

Any Ransom calls?

No.

Any Enemies?

No idea, if you or your government has any leads, please share it with us.

"Is there any similar case of kidnapping spiritual leaders happened in the past?", I asked.

She searched and investigated the computer records and responded, not recently but before 27 years there were several cases recorded during the time of International Spiritual Meet, hundreds of leaders were here out of them few went missing.

Is there any suspect behind this?

No, their cases are closed saying during that timeframe lot of people who come on tourist visa to America tear their documents and settled illegally here. It was assumed that these people also had followed similar methods in order to stay back in America. Search warrants were issued, but no luck. Since there were no ask or pressure from their government or from their near and dear ones seems we neither responded to anyone. The case went cold after few months.

Can I get a copy of that case file? She took a printout and handed over the same to me.

Look Mr. D we are giving our best to figure out what happened to Sadananda Guru. We are approaching this case in all possible aspects.

We will do our best. By the way please don't act on your own without proper orders. Let us know if you need anything from us.

Later she showed me the way out coming with me till the reception desk.

Just before I was about to leave, I asked her Can you do me a favour?

Yes, tell me?

Its personal, I would like to know what is inside these Floppy disks. Can you recover what's inside for me?

Smilingly she responded, this is a technology of past which our parents and grandparents used. The world has already moved on to flash drives and cloud, are you still playing with this toy? No worries I will have someone from my team look at this.

After saying goodbye, I left the FBI building. I called and updated my chief about the case status, got into a taxi, and reached home.

All the time on my way back I was thinking about what Mr. Singh told about my dad. Since my dad passed away even before I was born, all I remember is what my mother told about him. Beyond which I also didn't show interest in knowing more about him. Based on what Singh Sir narrated me, I wanted to know more about my father and what really happened to him.

After entering the house, I went through my father's leather bag once again. On opening a side zip, I found a journal. Yes, it was my father's journal.

I opened it searching the answers for Who is R.V? What kind of person he is? I turned the pages of the journal to know the answer in his own   words.

Journal

Vaidyalingam is a smalltime farmer in a village near Kumbakonam town. From morning 0600 AM to 0900 AM he completes all his farm duty and comeback to his home.

From 0900 AM he sit in the porch of his house and spend rest of the morning telling the astrology predictions for people visiting him with their horoscopes. Knowledge on Astronomy and astrology had been passed on to him from his previous generations. The predictions he makes will turn out 100 percent of the time correctly. The people in his village visits him often when they face hardships or for marriage horoscope matching or asking for auspicious day and time to start their business or housewarming to ensure good beginnings. Looking at the horoscope charts, If he finds there is a bad phase going on for a person which could turn worse, he asks them to light up Diya's to deities in nearby temple for 3 to 6 months or provide offerings to the needy and ask them to come back after that period.

Based on his experience he believes what he predicts will happen for sure. He also believes there is a science behind astrology, horoscopes and predictions and for some reasons it wasn't taught or lost I time when this skill was passed over multiple generations. If someone tries to pay him for his time, he refuses to accept it by saying it is a boon which was given to him by god. I should not use it to earn money. By god's grace I have a small land to farm, and I can make my living from that.

Baghya is his wife. Myself Rajesh I am their only son. When I was 8 years old my mom died suffering from a mystery fever. That moment I lost complete faith in god and my dad's Astro knowledge as they both could not help me save my mom.

My mom's dream is to make a responsible citizen in the society. From that day my dad took on that responsibility to groom me as one since it was his dearest wife's wish too.

I grew up as a charming, naughty, and intelligent kid. Science and Math came naturally to me as it was passed on to me genetically.

I grew my interest and passion towards science. I started questioning everything that can't be proved by science. I even questioned and mocked god and astrology.

Even though my father was surprised with my actions, he never forced his beliefs or his personal choices over me. He felt time would teach me various things in life through experiences.

I spent most of my time in the library reading articles on science magazine. I even went through the books and research papers written by Newton, Einstein, Rutherford, Feynman.

Knowing my interest is in science and math my teachers recommended me to pursue a degree in science. On completing my bachelors and master's in physics with distinction, I joined as a junior scientist in National Space Research Organization in Bangalore.

Around same time, I fell in love with Parvathy who is my cousin too. At least twice in a month I catch train from Bangalore to Kumbakonam to visit her and my father.

Years passed by, I felt disinterested and monotonous in the work I was doing. It had no relevance to what I wanted to work on. I came to know about an opening in another team which suited my interests. I asked my manager to change my team and role. He declined my move by responding, "Young chap, You should first complete Ph.D. if you want to be in such research roles".

So, I enrolled myself for a Ph.D. in Institute of science with their Quantum physics department. After Two and half years of balancing between work and studies, I finally managed to successfully defend my Ph.D. thesis on this subject. During 1990's there were only handful number of people around the world who is an expert in this topic.

Parvathy too had completed her degree and came to Bangalore as she got placed as a programmer in an IT company. From then, I stopped visiting my hometown other than for important festivals. Distance grew between my father and me. We speak over phone hardly once a week.

Everyday evening, I will take Parvathy in my bike for shopping, cinema, park, and temple. We enjoyed being in each other's company.

Few months later as expected there were research positions opened in the Quantum Computing team. This time there was a circular mentioning people having similar experience in relevant field internally can apply for this role. My skillsets and research work made me a candidate who is eligible for this job. I was one hundred percent confident in cracking the interview and get this role. I did the interview very well.

Weeks passed by; I was expecting the results from that interview. One fine afternoon my father had called me on my office landline number. I was surprised as mostly I am the one who would call him once a week.

Rajesh How are you doing? Do you have five minutes to speak?

Sure Dad.

Uncle and Aunt visited our house this morning. They want to get Parvathi married to you. They have handed over the horoscope of her to check the match.

"Ok Dad. What is your opinion?", I asked in excitement.

He answered, "What I am thinking is not to go ahead with this proposal. Being an educated person, you know it very well right, marrying a person within close relationship circle brings medical complications to next generations. So, I think of not going ahead with this proposal."

I felt like a lightning struck me to my core. Dad knows I am in serious love with Parvathy, then why is he saying like this.

After a pause, he went on and asked I hope you understand. Hope you are not disappointed?

Not knowing what to say, I ended the call saying, Dad seems my manager is calling me, shall we talk about this in the evening. I will call you once I reach home.

Once I ended the call, few minutes later I was asked to see the Manager for real. I thought it is going to be about the interview result. I ran to his room and knocked his door.

Seeing me, he asked me to get in and sit down. He went on saying "We recommended your application strongly for the position you had applied". Seems like your candidature didn't go through. So, you will be continuing in the same position. There will be future openings, you will get a chance next time.

There is a saying "Lightning never strikes twice". But to me it struck for second time within few minutes.

Not showing the disappointment, I asked him can I know who got selected for the roles?

I was told Umesh and Nayar got selected.

Hearing their name, not knowing how to show my disappointment, I responded saying, "Sir, they both were only having bachelor's degree. Moreover, they were 2 years junior to me too. To get into this lab I had worked hard and completed my Ph.D. It is my dream job. How is this possible Sir?"

Look Rajesh if you need further details you may have to speak with chairman sir. I was asked to communicate the result to you which I did. You may leave now.

On seeing me coming out disappointed friends questioned what's wrong?

I told them what happened. Immediately they responded this is a usual thing right, You should either come from the same state or butter up the superiors often. This will improve your chances to get selected to such positions. We have seen Umesh and Nayar worshiping the superiors like a hero which landed them this role. Tomorrow even if we reach those heights, we will think of having someone who is closer to us and trustworthy more than someone who deserves it right. If a chance is given to a deserving guy, then they would eventually become a threat to our position.

None of their words consoled me for my failure. I applied for leave for rest of the day and left home. I was torn between the thoughts from my father's earlier call and my failure to get the job I dreamt off. For the first time in my life, I felt the world is going against me.

I kicked and started my bike and went to Parvathi's office. The second I saw her approaching me, I asked her "Will you marry me?".

She replied without any thoughts, I will in this second.

Seeing the look at my face, she went on and asked why are you suddenly asking me this question?

Don't know what to say, I felt today is my worst day in life until I met you now.

I told without missing even a single word about what happened to me from the call I got from my father till the result I heard from my manager and comments made by my friends.

She consoled me saying, Don't worry Rajesh, we can go to Annamma Devi temple in Bangalore and can get married tomorrow itself. Also don't worry about the promotion, if not this there will be a better opportunity coming through your way.

I told her that I was under the impression the whole world is going against me until I met you now. But with you by my side I will win over anything.

Meeting her and sharing my feelings, I felt lot relaxed. Didn't notice the time as we lost ourselves in the conversation. Suddenly she noticed the time and asked me can I drop her back to her accommodation. We had dinner in our favorite restaurant, and I dropped her back to her place. When I was about to leave, she commented saying please be there on time in the temple for Marriage tomorrow. I left the place with a light heart.

I reached the quarters, collected mails from the mailbox and entered the house. My landline phone kept ringing. I took the receiver and answered the call with a Hello.

It was my Father on the other side. He enquired about the matter we spoke in the morning. When he was about to say something, I interrupted him and told openly that I am very much in love with Parvathi, please get us married.

Being a girl's life involved my father opened-up and shared the truth.

Rajesh, when I was analyzing the match between your horoscopes, if this marriage happens at most you will live together for 3 years.

I responded saying I don't believe in astrology, but I know from my school days a word coming out of your mouth certainly had happened. Could you please be specific? Is there a problem for anyone with this marriage?

Yes, as per your charts, if you get married to any girl at the most you will be alive for only 3 years. You are going to face your worst fear that could take away your life. That is why I was against this marriage from the beginning. No father would want even to hear that his son will be dead.

You think straight and let me know what your opinion on this matter is. I will accept what you are going to say. Saying these words, he ended the call.

Inside him he knew very well this marriage is going to happen and his fears are going to come true.

I was in totally confused state, after a deep thinking throughout the night, when the day broke, I decided to break-up with Parvathi. Since I could not stand a thought, she would be suffering in my absence. I don't even want to imagine her in that state.

I stopped picking any calls or meeting her for the next few days. I missed her badly, my love for her made me cry inside my heart. I could not concentrate on my work. I roamed the city like a clueless person.

On the other side, Parvathi didn't know why I am ignoring her or not responding to her calls. Seems she came to my office directly where she was told I am on leave. Thought something is wrong she came to my Quarters and waited there to meet me form morning 1000AM till evening. Around 0830 PM on hearing my bike sound she came to the gate.

When I stopped my vehicle and turned back, I saw her approaching me and slapping at my face. Next second filled with tears in our eyes, we hugged each other. She even threw some punches on my chest. Why did you avoid me? Where were you from this morning? She had train of questions coming on my way.

With the heavy heart I told the truth.

She responded, "I am telling you for the last time, if I am going to get married it will be with you". Come this second, we can go and get married. She stood there filled with tears in her eyes.

That is the moment we knew we can't live without each other, we decided to get married. We got married in the most prominent Annamma Devi temple in Bangalore with our parent's blessings. We started and led our life very happily.

Two months after marriage, when we were organizing the home, Parvathi came across a sealed letter. Showing it to me she asked what is this letter?

I took It from her and was curious to go through the message without knowing it contained a life changing message for me.

Breakthrough

I opened the letter and started reading it. It's a call letter from US Embassy in Chennai. One of America's greatest company Research Labs had gone through my credentials and proficiency in Quantum physics discipline and asked for a meeting with me. It also had a message to reach out to a phone number in the back to make necessary arrangements.

Research Labs, a top tier scientific research organization specializing in predicting what are the technologies that is going to rule the world in next twenty to thirty years and start working on that today to make it a reality. Every scientist craves to be part of that organization. Seeing a call letter from one such organization that too in an Embassy building, I was over enthusiastic and immediately called the number provided on the letter.

Over the call I shared the details and fixed the date and time for my meeting. In next two days they had sent me a first-class train ticket from Bangalore to Chennai along with a hotel booking for my stay.

The day of meeting came. I went through security screening first before reaching the front desk. I showed the call letter I had received. The lady in the front office took a note and asked me to be seated.

After five minutes she came with a security personnel and told me he would be escorting me. After walking across the campus and climbing few stairs he finally asked me to get inside one of the conference rooms.

While I was about to enter, I noticed two women already present in the room. In her own accent, One of them introduced herself as Madame Olivia Mayhem Chief Executive Officer for Research labs. Then she went ahead and introduced the lady next to her as Carla Officer in charge with US Embassy in Chennai.

Do you know why did we call you here?

I said, "No".

Our Lab's chief scientist Alan had gone through your research articles in International Journals for Quantum physics and computing. He was really impressed with your knowledge and understanding of this domain.

The topic you had done your research is a special one. We can count number of people with such proficiency in this domain.

The power of inventing such a computer and computing technology is going to be a boon to mankind. We have many plans to on making it work. The purpose we called you here is, I am inviting you to America to work with us for the role of director in our new quantum computing lab. This is once in a lifetime opportunity.

Moreover, here is your green card application and other offer details. We will also sponsor your dependents too. Take a look and you can decide and let us know your decision in next 3 days. We will proceed accordingly from there. They left the room saying bye for now, see you soon in America.

I was under the impression whether I was in a dream or living the dream.

With full joy and excitement, I vacated the room and left for Bangalore same day. After reaching home I shared the experience and details of the meeting with Parvathi.

I hugged and kissed her, later praised her saying your words came true. I haven't dreamt of such an opportunity even once.

Having said this good news, she asked where is the Sweet.

Not only sweet, but we will also go for a treat tomorrow.

OK, What do you think of this opportunity? Should I take this offer? Are you ready to go and live in America?

I got one response for all my questions. I want you to be happy and if working there is going to make you the happiest man I am ready to fly tomorrow?

What about your Job?

That is ok, It's been a year hardly I had been in this role. I can go and find a suitable job after going there.

Great, I will say ok to this offer tomorrow morning itself. With the thoughts of "landing in a dream job that too with an exciting offer of getting a green card in America, being one in a billon getting such opportunity", circling in my mind I couldn't sleep well that night.

After two months of preparation and blessings from family members we both reached America. A guest house was arranged for us to stay for the first month.

My first day in office I went and met Mercy. I was calling her Mam after every other sentence. She asked me to stop calling Mam and asked me to call her MOM from the initials of her name **Mercy Olivia Mayhem**. She went on and said we will also call you RV (Rajesh Vaidyalingam) from now on.

She took me to most of the departments and introduced me to her team and staff. Later she told her secretary to help me with my questions on bank account opening, Insurance and Immigration.

I was given an office car, flexible work timing, enough leaves as benefits. Days ran faster as I got into this new Job. We gave birth to a Baby girl. We named her Lakshmi after goddess of wealth as we were blessed with abundant wealth along with her birth.

There were only 2 Indian nationals including me working in that campus. I happened to connect with the Cafeteria Manager Mr. Singh who is an Indian national. We became close friends as days passed. I bought and moved to a new house in the community next to the home where Mr. Singh and his family lived.

We invited my father and In-laws and celebrated our daughter's first birthday vary grandly.

Singh Sir's and my family, we bonded like real brothers and sisters. We go to picnics together, if one our family member is unwell food will be prepared from other home and shared. Our kids were also playmates. They eat and sleep in the same house where they were playing on that day.

Once Mr. Singh required six thousand US dollars to renew his cafeteria contract for next ten years. He felt to himself asking me, I would feel like exploiting the friendship. So, he went around and met people and friends from his circles to help him. But everything went in vain. If he could not renew the license, he might have to close his business and go back to India.

When I came to know about the situation, I was angry at him first, since as a friend he didn't even let me know, he needed money. I avoided him for next few days. Knowing something is wrong he stopped me saying Array!!! RV Bhai, what is wrong with you? Why are you avoiding me?

I responded with anger, I treated you as more than my friend, I considered you as my brother, why did you hide your requirement from me. Did you think I won't help you? Here is the cheque for Six thousand dollars. Please take it.

Mr.Singh hesitated at first. I told him I am not giving this money for free. You must give it back to me in six months. He took the cheque from me, laughed, and hugged me with tears.

I had a selfish reason too, as he is my only friend who had stood with me during all times. But Mr. Singh is man of words, exactly on Sixth month he returned the money he had borrowed from me. Years passed by.

Everything was picture perfect in my life until that Saturday. After hectic road trips, picnics and celebrations, I went to office to complete my pending office works. I could see very few heads on the weekend. On my way to my desk, I found an ID card on the hallway. It was none other than Alan our Chief Scientist's Identity card. I though he might have missed it I scanned his card and entered his office to hand it over to him. I advanced into his lab calling his name.

It was the first time I came into his office. On my way something interesting I found on his table. Those were copy of my research papers I had published in International Journals.

Calling his name, I went slightly forward. I noticed a presentation in his computer. After looking into that, I learnt why people say curiosity kills the cat. What I had seen in his computer screen shocked me. It raised my heartbeat and shot my blood pressure. More to that the scenes I saw there froze my blood and I went into a total state of shock.

Few minutes later I came to my senses, I took my camera out of my bag and took photograph of what I saw there. I came out of his room immediately and went to mine. I could not concentrate on my work. I was totally confused of what I saw in Alan's office. I sensed something wrong is going there and left the office. On my way back I handed over Alan's card to the lost and found desk and asked them to hand it over to him.

The Journal ended there with empty pages from that point. Thinking hard of what my dad could have seen there actually and what could have gone wrong to him, I fell asleep.

Murders

Next day morning when I woke up, all my family were getting ready to go back to Pittsburgh. Citing my work, I decided to stay in the New York city for next few days. I told them I would ask for an accommodation from my office.

Bharath responded saying why you must stay outside. Feel free to stay in our home here.

I said Ok and send them off. It's been a week no news about Sadananda Guru. FBI and police here were not allowing me to act in my way. Pressure was put up from my department.

I was about to leave for FBI office to join them in their investigation, my phone rang. Call is from Asha, upon answering the call, she said in a tense voice can you come quickly to my office. Please be there as soon as possible.

I said yes and took a taxi immediately and reached the FBI office. Asha was waiting for me, and she took me to a conference room with big screens. She asked her team member to project the details.

She continued, "You know what?" These are the same people from the additional case files I shared with you the other day. We recovered it from the disks you gave it to us other day. Around eighteen of them have been murdered cruelly. They tore apart their back and left their flesh open. There were some more files in the disc which were encrypted. Experts are working to decrypt them and see what is in there.

"D", I think there could be some connection between this and our current case.

I asked her, "Any Suspect?"

Not for sure, we might have got his visual. While he was photographing this there was an image of him from the reflection in the glass windows. Initial conclusion is he is an Asian men could be in his early thirties looking at the timelines of cases that reported these people went missing. We have brought in our experts to improve the image and recognize his face. Once the work is done, we will run his profile in our database. If needed, we will publish it to the news, so we can get some leads about his whereabouts.

As she spoke with me, she showed me the not so clear image of that person. I was totally shocked to see it. Reason is, the person I saw in that image was my own father's face.

Asha tapped my shoulders and brought me to senses and went on asking questions, "Are you alright? Do you know him by any chance?"

I replied, "No, I was in to thinking how this case is relevant to ours now".

Can you send me the copy of the report and the image? I will also ask my people to search for his profile in our department database.

Sure, I had sent you the image to your phone. By the way, D where did you get these evidence?

Not knowing how to answer her, I simply told her someone threw me this inside the car I was travelling while I was on my way to your office the very first day. I didn't know what's inside and that is why asked your help. Also, until you called me today, I didn't know this evidence has got such a material.

"By the way, we got some anonymous tips about the whereabouts of Sadananda guru. Some one had seen the people who abandoned that Ambulance on that old bridge the other day. I am going there to enquire them; would you like to join?", Asha asked me.

I said Yes and went with her to three to four places, but nothing concrete turned up.

After saying Bye, I once again came back to home. I kept looking at my father's journal and the images which Asha sent me this morning. I could not connect how are they related. Why my father should have these photograph in his belongings.

Who my father is? Is he really a cold-blooded murderer? If I share the details I know so far to FBI and if it makes the news, My mom would be even worried to know about my fathers another face. I could not think straight how to move forward.

Suddenly Mythili came into my room asking, "Seems you returned so soon. What are you staring at your screen?"

She looked at my phone screen and asked me how do you know him?

I was shocked to hear it from her and responded to her, "why are you asking me this question?"

No, he looks like Uncle John. The person in that image. That is why I asked you?

Wait, Can you come again? Have you seen him before? Do you know him?

The person in the photo looked like Uncle John. It looks like it was taken when he was young. But not so sure.

Where have you seen him?

He runs a restaurant near the university where me and my brother graduated.

That is when I recalled Bharath enquiring about John, when Bharath took me to that restaurant for the first time.

If Uncle John is My father? How is he related to all these murders? Why should he change his identity and live? I recalled the conversation where the waiter responded to Bharath saying John and Mary went to New York for hearing the speech of some spiritual guru that day.

If I connect the dots, my father must have abducted Sadananda Guru too. He could be doing the same mistake which he committed twenty-five years back. I need to know the truth and stop this somehow. I should first go to that restaurant and meet John.

Mythili, can you take me to John's restaurant in Pittsburgh. It is little urgent.

She was clueless but wanted to help me, so she said yes.

We both left for Pittsburgh, on our way I slowly opened up about the situation I am currently in. She was shocked at first but went on and told, "I have known Uncle John and his restaurant from student days. He is really a nice person; I don't think he has any dark secrets or past as you imagine. John and Mary sister both were running the restaurant for almost twenty years. I think your intuition is wrong. Don't worry you will have the answers as we are going to meet him in few more hours".

It was around half past eleven when we reached the restaurant. They were about to close the restaurant; I saw a waiter cleaning up the table. When I was about to enter the restaurant Asha called to my phone.

Asha went on "D we identified the suspect, his name is R.V., But he is no more, seems like he died in a kitchen fire accident, seems like gas explosion. But we are digging more about his family".

On hearing it I got nervous and shocked.

Where are you now? Can you tell the truth from where you got these evidence?

My phone battery died and got switched off when Asha was interrogating me with above questions.

Meanwhile Asha got angry as she tried to reach D several times in the interim, but D could not respond since his phone battery died. Why should he switch off his phone? D made into her suspect list, but she thought if D is really involved in this case, how come he will voluntarily hand over a crucial evidence to her. Does he know more than what our department knows. Is he trying to act on his own? So, she asked her deputy to track his cellphone and find where D is and follow him. If needed she asked him to be ready to take him in custody on her orders.

True Self

As I was curious to know who John really is, I thought of calling Asha later and entered the restaurant. I saw a charging cable near a table in which I started charging my phone. I approached the waiter and asked him can I see John?

Waiter responded, "John is not here, he mentioned he has some other personal work and left early". Mostly he will come tomorrow morning. If you can come tomorrow, you can meet him.

It is little urgent? Can you tell me where he has gone?

Sorry I don't know. But here is his phone number. You can talk to him directly.

I took Mythili's phone and started calling him. A phone started vibrating near the cashier's desk. Waiter noticed it and told seems John had left his phone on this desk. You should come tomorrow If you have to meet him.

I asked him we have travelled so far; can we have some thing to drink or eat.

We have already closed our kitchen's. Let me see if we have some milk, so I can prepare a tea. You can take some snack from that desk.

When the waiter went inside to prepare some tea, I took John's cell phone and went through his phone records. It was an older model of cellphone not even having touch screen or display. So, no photos. It wasn't locked either. Upon scrolling his caller list, I saw calls received from several merchants. There were few calls from Mary and the most recent one was from my brother-in-law Bharath.

I heard the waiter's footsteps approaching, I dropped the phone back and came back to my table. Mythili and me both drank some tea and ate the snack and decided to come next day morning. It was around 0200 AM in the morning when we reached home. On seeing our car headlamp my mother opened the doors for us.

Mythili was extremely tired due to long drive and fell asleep on the couch as soon as we entered.

Mom asked, "Why are you guys here all of a sudden, why haven't you informed us?"

I replied, "It was my work which brought me here". I asked Mythili to drive me here.

We heard the toddler crying in the next room. Mom told I think Baby is hungry and he will wake up, I will go and attend him, let us talk in the morning. Before going to her room, she took a blanket and covered Mythili.

I went into my room; due to tiredness I fell asleep. When I woke up it was almost Eleven in the morning. I refreshed myself and got ready to meet John. When I went downstairs, Mythili was still sleeping. I asked my sister can you call for a taxi.

D, you can drive here with your Indian license. You can take either my car or Mythili's. But be careful, the steering wheel is on the left-hand side and you have to keep right side on the roads.

I took Mythili's car key and asked my sister where Bharat is.

Sister replied, "You both came here without telling us. Bharath went to New York to meet some people for his project."

I went on and asked, "He just came from there a week before? Anything important?

Seems so, the algorithm he has been researching seems complete. But he doesn't have the facility here to test it. So, he requested the company he gave interview too in the last week to host him to allow him to use their facility. Seems he got the approval from the CEO. That is why he went back.

Mom intervened and said, "D Have some food for your breakfast?"

No mom I am going on an urgent work, I will have it there.

Mom replied, "Ok".

When I was about to leave a question popped into my head. How come being in the same city Sister didn't get to meet John. I went ahead and asked her, have you eaten in the Indian restaurant Bharath took me the other day?

She responded, "No dude, My office commute is 65 miles from her to downtown. Bharath's university is 90 miles from here in the opposite direction. Bharath used to call me on weekends but didn't find a chance yet to visit". Why are you asking?

No, nothing, I simply asked.

I took Mythili's car and drove on the wrong side, upon hearing the honks I corrected my position in the road.

After an hour of drive I reached the Restaurant. I felt like someone is tailing me, purely my police instinct. I parked my car and went inside the restaurant to know the real face of John.

On entering inside I saw the same waiter whom I met last night. He came to me and handed me over phone I left there charging.

I took the phone from him, switched it on and asked can I meet John, it is little urgent.

Waiter replied "Sorry, he is busy in the Kitchen. Please wait here, I will inform him."

After 5 minutes, some one patted my back asking how can I help you gentleman?

When I turned, I saw a man with French beard, spectacles, jean pant, T-shirt and scars on his hand and face most probably due to a fire accident. On seeing the face, I was totally shocked. I recalled the photo of my father with same face we have in our home.

On seeing me his face went pale, since I resembled my mom. I think I might have reminded my mom.

John asked me, "who are you? ". Same moment, I received a call from Asha.

John asked me to answer the call first.

The moment I accepted the call, Asha was fuming and firing, What do you think you are doing? Why are you with the murderer RV? What are you both scheming together? We know he is your father. Both of you please surrender immediately.

While I was busy thinking how she found where I am, I turned my head on all direction. I saw a young man in a coat pretending to be eating, but he kept his eye on me.

I ended the call immediately and asked my Dad, is there another way from here to get out.

Why, Who are you in first place? my father asked.

He was confused as I responded to him that I am his son.

Don't play, I don't have a family. Tell me who you are really?

I promise you; I am your son; My mother is Parvathi.

On hearing my mother's name, he said What are you blabbering?

I could hear a police vehicle siren approaching from a long distance, I know it was Asha who would have sent police to arrest us. I asked him once again is there another way to exit this building.

Not knowing what to say he took me inside the kitchen and showed a way out from there.

I asked him to join with me.

Without knowing police is there to arrest him he responded saying why should I come with you?

I saw a van used to carry goods for the restaurant with the key inside it. I pushed my father into the van, locked the door and started the van to escape from that place.

On the way he kept asking, "Who are you? Why are you doing this? Please drop me here else I will jump from the running vehicle.

A call came from Asha once again. I put the call on Speaker.

Asha continued, "How dare you both? Despite my warning, you and RV are trying to escape.

On hearing his real name, my father was shocked. He calmed down for the first time and started listening to me.

I asked Asha for few hours and promised we both will surrender.

I don't know D; We are tracking you; we will keep searching for you. You can't escape anywhere. We will have you in our custody within next 12 hours else both of you will be on the headlines. I can't help you.

Feeling helpless, I turned the vehicle from the main road to inside village road. The vehicle got broke down after few miles. We left the vehicle there. I took out the sim card from my phone and broke it and kept my phone switched off so they could not track it with my IMEI number.

We both got into a bus which came on our way and got down in a nearest market.

My father took me inside a shop he knew well in that market. He asked me to stop playing and asked me to tell the truth?

How come did you know I am RV?

I told him the truth and the reason why I and mother are in US.

He touched my cheeks for a second and then took back his hand. He asked me, "Why are the police chasing you now?"

I replied, "Infact police is searching for you for the eighteen murders you committed earlier. More importantly what have you done with Sadananda Guru? Why did you kidnap him?"

What are you accusing me off, Did I commit murders? Did I kidnap Sadananda guru?

I didn't understand my father response, as he was totally denying the allegations, I kept against him. I told him about my meeting with Mr. Singh earlier in the week and the bag he handed over to me. As a matter of fact, the floppy disks inside your bag revealed the evidence and brough to light that you are a cold-blooded murderer. This is the reason the police are chasing you now.

I went on and vented, I could not believe how my mom believed you and kept telling us you are a really a good person all these years. If you haven't done these murders, why did you change your identity and living in hiding. Why haven't you tried reaching police or mom or grandparents. I once again accused him saying you are a selfish and cold-blooded murderer.

Core Theme

As he could not stand my accusations, he slapped me and asked me to stop.

Do you want to know the truth which I have buried with in me for these twenty-five years? Do you know how much pain I am suffering from in missing my dearest wife and daughter? Common, listen to it.

Common spill the truth, I will listen? I replied in anger.

My father continued…

That day what I saw in the lab shook me to my core. I went totally numb for few minutes. Once I came to my home, the whole incident was playing in my mind continuously. I was searching for answers to all the questions that came up in my mind. Why Alan did a thing like this in first place?

Several of Hindu Gurus, Sufi saints, Buddhist monks, Zen masters, Jew Rabbi's and other spiritual gurus who came for an international spiritual meet went missing. What are they doing inside Alan's lab? Why are some of their body found split open from the back. Few of them were placed in chiller boxes.

How is my paper and research related to these? How is the algorithm I am going to submit in another two weeks going to get used? Whatever I have been told so far is it a purely a lie?

For real what am I doing here?

I investigated the photographs and documents I collected in the lab. Something sparked me. There was a paper of mine which talks about how human brains function is similar to a Quantum computer functioning. If one can understand how the human brain works achieves such a potential, we can mimic a quantum computer. I learnt finally they were trying to design a quantum computer through this research.

You can ask me what's so special about that quantum computer?

If we have one such computer, we can solve all the world's complex problems which can't be algorithmically solved by our today's classical computer for next hundreds of years.

If we can come out with a stable design of quantum computer, we can get answers for all the following questions.

It has the power to analyze the human genes and understand which sequence of the genes are related to longevity of life either we can find out drugs to increase the longevity or else we can perform gene editing when the fetus is in the womb and create a species which has more longevity.

It has the power to understand the chemical composition of all the drugs and how those individual molecules help in fighting against a diseased cell. Once we know how this works through simulations, we can create effective medicine for any deadly disease going forward.

It had the power to analyze and bring to light the characteristics of all the elements in periodic table and how do they exactly react when combined with each other. Simulating and knowing this using a classical computer will take thousands of years. But with quantum computers we can do it at ease and use the findings to create a low weight, strong and long-lasting alloy which could be put to human use.

It has the power to create an artificial chemical fertilizer which won't impact the soil quality or poison the crops and the ecosystem around it

It has the power to improve the efficiency of solar cells and batteries, so we can move to highly efficient renewable source of energy.

It has the power to crack any passwords in fraction of a second, One can use such computers in defense forces to detect and overcome cyber-attacks or to destroy incoming missiles.

Lastly, once can simulate the process of photosynthesis and understand the exact chemical reaction that breaks down Carbon dioxide to Oxygen. If we understand the mechanism well, we can create artificial leaves that could get enough oxygen around us.

In short, a computer like this would help us leave the World a better place for future generations to come.

I wanted to be part of the team who achieves it. To be frank it would give me a feeling of god as I can create all the above said wonders. To achieve this, I did my Ph.D. in this domain. America welcomed me with red-carpet as there were only handful of people researching on this topic then.

Once I joined Research Labs, I was happy to be part of something big which is going to be helpful for this mankind. I really felt proud of where I have come in my career.

During 1990's, what ever I told above was just in papers and literatures. Purely a theory. Lot of big companies had invested in Research labs to make these technologies come true. Building one such computer of that capability and operating them with proper set of instructions was a tedious task. This is when I learnt Alan tried to reproduce my theoretical understanding of human brain function similarity with quantum world.

You can ask me what is so brilliant in my paper.

Quantum computer bits are designed using chemicals such as phosphorous by converting them into their ion stage. Ions are nothing but charged atomic particles. Several such electrically charged ions are trapped. These trapped ions are called quantum bits analogous to transistor made bits in classical computers, but the mechanics of logical operations performed on them totally different. Light source is passed over these trapped ions and measurements are performed to get a solution to the problem. But the challenge is to get these ions trapped and maintaining them to be in a stable condition. Alan's lab was researching in developing one such quantum computer.

My research articles summarized how humans in the past has turned themselves in to a quantum computer. They achieve it through meditation. The breathing pattern of a person who is meditating gets stabilized first. It then ionizes the phosphorous and calcium atoms present in the Cerebro spinal fluid. Through constant practice these ions start from our root chakra and reach up to the human brain. Once these ions get stabilized in the brain then the light from within spreads over the neuron's cells, DNA and these ions. As we meditate on certain topic the information stored in our DNA and Neuron cells are triggered, combined, and combed together through these neuron-ion circuits and one end up getting clarity of thought or answer for their questions from within. Some people relate this to Kundalini or the serpent power. Some people relate this to enlightenment.

But Biology behind this is simple, breathing ionizes the Cerebro spinal fluid and these are those ions which improve our cognitive power as it moves upwards and stabilize near our brain. Based on the methods and practice the strength and stability of these ions differ giving rise to different levels of clarity of thoughts. Spiritual gurus of those days had achieved such state where their brain remained as a quantum computer.

This quality in them helped them to present their views clearly during discourses, Q&A or through debates.

My article summarized if we would be able to understand how this phenomenon happens in the humans, one can get the formulae to make a quantum computer or turn themselves in to one.

I doubted why Alan and his team might not have tried to experiment on these spiritual leaders to understand this phenomenon. I went through the files in his computers. My doubt got confirmed. I could see the readings and measurements made about the breathing patterns when still and during meditation. To add to this, I also found the images where probes are inserted in their spinal regions to track the movement of ions. It sees they have given pain killers to cut open their back and insert those probes at right places.

People who could not tolerate the pain or accidentally died during this process is put inside a chiller box. It is the scene I saw when I entered Alan's lab other day.

My contribution in this entire research was to come up with an efficient computing algorithm required to perform necessary computations with the quantum computer. I almost got the initial breakthrough and was ready to test my algorithm in the coming weeks.

Connecting all the dots, I finally concluded why they have pushed me to accelerate my research. Moreover, I questioned myself who had authorized such dangerous experiments to be performed.

Fight or Flight

I spent my weekend thinking about this totally. I felt like not going to that office anymore. I felt I indulged myself in a bigger scheme of criminal activity. I didn't even speak well with my wife and daughter. I collected all the details regarding this research in floppy disks and planned to go to police.

My wife came running to me in Joy and said, "I am going to give you good news".

Our telephone rang. She went and picked it up.

It was MOM on the other end. She asked my wife to give the phone to me.

Parvathi passed the phone to me. I got the phone from her and said Hello and the very next second MOM blasted me saying "What have you done RV? Please report to the office immediately. We must talk.

Reason for her anger is I entered the Export control technology lab. Only the citizens of US can enter in to Export controlled blue zones. That is the reason access is controlled for those doors. Whereas my citizenship application is still under processing. In few week time me and my family would have granted the citizenship from the immigration department and be accepted as citizens.

I left to my office campus immediately and went to MOM's office. I could see some new faces in the same room.

She started, "RV you know the rules and regulations of this office, then why did you do this?"

When I was struggling for an explanation, she went on and said we know you know the truth. We could see from the CCTV records and lab access records you had entered Alan's export-controlled technology lab. To add to that you tried to hack into Alan's system and snooped into his files.

MOM, I didn't do anything intentionally. If you permit, I would like to resign my job and go back to my country. I feel something is not right and I don't want to be part of it. If you won't allow, I have no other choice other than going to police and tell them what I have seen.

It's impossible RV. You have known more details than you should. You got yourself involved in bigger scheme of things. This would cause a big damage to us. Here is our damage control proposal. To contain the damage, I order you to complete your research as soon as possible and join Alan in his lab. Only if you agree we will recommend on your citizenship application. Then everything will be back to normal.

Else we would file a case against you stating you were here to steal the secrets of this land and you were trying to sell it to antinational elements and forces. You will have to face lifetime jail for this fraud. Your family also will be punished for conspiring with you. We have all the evidence to frame you on this case.

By the way, please meet lawyers from Bee group. They are our investors. We are partnering with them to deliver your research outcomes. You have known things which are supposed to remain secrets, so hear this too from your research we are planning on to create a precision attack weapons and also hack and control nuclear weapons, also we were planning to create some biological organism that would attack humans and we will use the same research to find the cure and sell it for high price. In the upcoming internet era, we plan to create disturbances to finance sectors by hacking their system with this Quantum computer and algorithm

To put it in a nutshell we are going to rule the world!!! We will have the power to decide who should live and who should die.

MOM - How can you do this? It is insane, pure madness. I will not cooperate with you on this anymore.

R.V. all these things what I told you, I am not going to do it. It will be you who will help us achieve this. You know them as investors, but for sure they can make or break you career not only that your entire life too. Uttering this words, she broke the pencil in her hand in to two. Laughing at me see said, Do you want to see your family dead when you return home today? Are you asking for it?

Get out of my office now and get back to your work. You have no other choice.

When I was about to get out of her office, those lawyers told me they will catch up with me after a smoking break.

Not knowing they sent people to follow me, I went into the cafeteria.

I was totally disappointed and went into a deep thinking. I aspired to contribute to uplift quality of life for mankind through my research whereas there is a plan to totally use it for illegal purposes. The thoughts of wellbeing of my family came before me. At what cost I don't want anything bad to happen to anyone.

Looking me sad, Mr. Singh came to my table and asked should I get 3 tea. Why he is asking 3, I am just one person. Confusingly I turned my head behind and realized there were two guards who had already started following me.

I ignored them and asked for a tea. In the nick of the moment got an idea and went with my bag to Cashiers desk. I told to Mr. Singh I got into a very big trouble. I need your help. I requested him to help my family members to leave the country and get to India on the plane same day. Also tell them I will be joining them in another two to three days.

From my voice, he understood partially and promised me to that he will take care of it. Out of tensions I left my bag on is desk and left to my office.

Mr. Singh reached out to his friends and managed to get two tickets to India. He carried the tickets to RV's home and asked them to get ready stating some emergency in their family. I handed over the tickets to them.

Parvathi looked at the tickets and asked why is there only two tickets?

Due to last minute emergency, I was able to arrange only two tickets. Mr. Singh replied.

By the way, please pack the required things and get ready, we should leave in another two hours.

Parvathi could not understand what is going on. She called her parents and Father-in-law. No luck to reach them. She called me in my office number. I plainly stated them to leave as soon as possible taking Mr. Singh's help and promised them I will join them in next 2 days. I said to them I will discuss more on this once you reach India. I ended the call soon as I have been followed and tracked.

Families bid goodbye and Mr. Singh took them to Airport. He was with them till they complete their check-in process and advanced to their gate. He collected our Parents number from Parvathi and informed them about their arrival. So, they will be there to pick them when then land in Bangalore. He made sure they boarded the flight through the status displays in the airports. Finally, he came back to office and sent me a note along with tea to my room. I felt slightly relaxed as I could save them from any immediate danger.

I left for the day to my home with those two guards following me. When I came to parking lot, I saw Mr. Singh for the last time. I thanked him bowing myself with folded hands as I didn't want to talk to him and get him and his family into the mess, I am in.

I roamed in my garden thinking what I should do next. I thought of telling the truth to police and dialed 3 times and ended the call before someone picked up. I finally decide to go to police station with all the evidence. That is when I realized I had left my evidence bag on the cashier's table in the cafeteria.

It seems MOM learnt my family had already left America. She also learnt I am going to take the truth to public. So, she arranged a hit man to kill me.

If I go and meet Mr. Singh, it will create unnecessary trouble for him. I tried calling him over phone. Some one had disconnected my phone line by then. They took out the fuse of my electricity board. The house went dark. Both the guards who followed me and stationed near my home were taken back.

I could feel someone in my home. I thought of leaving the place, so I took my car key and went to garage.

Next day morning in the Newspaper they declared me dead due to Gas blast accidentally. They could not get my remains as the entire house was burnt.

Without knowing whom I am fighting against, I almost lost everything. I only had two choices, in front of me either to fight against them legally which is not possible given their strength or to take a flight. I chose the second one to Fly, to go absconding or live in hiding with the world knowing I am dead with the satisfaction of saving my family at least.

How come they published the news stating you are dead when you are alive?

I tried to leave the home and entered my garage. That time the hit man gave a strong blow with a rod from my behind. I struggled hard to fight against him. I lost my ring finger in the struggle. Finally, I overpowered him and gave him a strong blow. He fell unconscious. I saw a message coming to his pager as it vibrated. I took it from his pocket and read the message which said "Kill R.V.".

I thought of leaving the place as soon as possible to save myself. When I went to open the car door, the hitman gained consciousness and hit me once again strongly. I fell coughing with blood in my mouth. I could not even move an inch. But I didn't decide to die and wanted to live badly, so I gained all my strength and gave a strong blow in his chest. When he struggled to get up, I kicked him hardly which took him close to kitchen. The explosives he brought to set it up in my home to kill me blew up. Since he fell near to kitchen the gas also blew up and I was thrown away several meters from the house. Just based on the ring finger they found in the garage I was declared dead. It took few weeks for me to come to senses and gain strength to walk. I tried reaching Parvathi, my father, and my in-laws several times. No one had picked the call, after few weeks I received a tone saying these numbers were permanently disconnected. Not knowing about their whereabouts or their state I cried for years to date.

I consoled my father and told, "I remember hearing from my grand father that my entire family relocated to support my mother as she got a job and relocated to Chennai after two weeks of father's death. More to this he also had mentioned someone close to our family gave the news of my mom and sister arriving to Bangalore and the same person passed on the news of my father's death. They had opened the news to their daughter as soon as she arrived. She fainted in front of Airport and was taken to hospital and got admitted for 2 days.

Mother kept crying ,saying her husband can't even tolerate a small heat. How would he have felt when the entire fire engulfed him. She was even more that worried he left this world without even knowing they are going to become parents once again.

Months rolled over; she gave birth to me. All the grief and sadness that stuck my house until then flew away. It was a magic I brought with me at least that is what my grandparents told me. Her husband's wish was to bring up her daughter a more independent kid with all the skills she aspires for. My mom took it as her aim and started living her life from scratch. With the help of her Parents and income from her Job she gave us a good education and brough up as a responsible kids. My sister became a software programmer like my mom and moved to America for the job. I on the other side completed my engineering and took up a role in Uniform services. My family was so proud of me and my sister. My mom hid all her suffering behind her to make us where we are today.

Suddenly the name Mary struck me. I asked my father who Mary is.

He started answering. When I survived the fire accident, I took the bus which came my way and reached Pittsburgh. When I got down muggers took away my purse, money, and gold ornaments I wore. When I woke up, I saw Mary and her husband had given me first aid.

When I came to consciousness, they asked me who I was? Thinking of hiding the truth I told them an agent took me to US on a tourist visa claiming he will get me a job. Once I landed, he took all my money and documents and left me. They were convinced with my reason as it happened commonly over there.

Mary Sister's husband is a Lawyer. He helps the refuges to get asylum visa. He also helps them by getting them a job as driver, hotel guard or restaurant waiters to restart their life. He is really a good men except an alcoholic. In fact, he asked me to apply for the asylum visa, since there were no biometrics those days, they could not verify my identity and granted me the visa. He also got me a job in a restaurant.

After few years, Mary sister's husband died of damages to his organs due to alcohol consumption. Mary sister collected all her savings and decided to start a small restaurant in her house for her survival. She called me and offered me the job since I had some experience by then. We worked very hard to make it the way it is today. Over time she considered me as her brother.

My father completed his story and asked, "Ok how is your mother and sister doing now? Can you take me to them? I want to see them for one time. I have been longing for this day."

I got a thought what kind of person is he, who hasn't even shown his affection to his son when I was near him, but he cares more about his wife and daughter.

I realized since I was not brought up by him, neither him nor me had any attachments or affection other than respect for each other.

I thought if I can prove my father is not guilty based on what he told and take him infront of my mother, how happy she would be.

To his question I responded No explaining him if we go there now, we will be unnecessarily dragging the whole family in to the mess we are today. I added first we will go to New York and meet Asha there. We will let here know what happened and cooperate with her on the investigations and come out clean.

With the help of one of the truck driver in the same market we started our journey to New York.

Return of the evil

It was a snowy day. Seems like a blizzard was over the previous day. Roads were empty. Around 0400 AM in the morning MOM, Alan and a small group had assembled in the Quantum Research Labs.

In a fully secured premise, they entered the room where they had held Sadananda guru. They had attached lots of probes covering his entire body starting from his head, chest, spines, back and legs.

With help of those they were measuring and recording various body parameters such as heart rate, blood pressure levels, brain waves, breathing pattern, Cerebro Spinal fluid state, Magnetic field around him.

They were forcing him to perform meditations by giving instructions from adjacent rooms.

Sadananda guru resisted to oblige them.

MOM got furious and spoke over the microphone, Listen Guru, we approached you formally to conduct some experiments on you. You had refused it. Look what happened. You are in our custody today. Even now we are requesting you to cooperate with us. Years before when we had very fewer imaging facilities, we did brutal inhuman experiments on spiritual leaders.

Now with the advent of facilities we are using the most recent imaging systems to scan your brain, spine to know what changes happen in you as you practice.

If you fail to cooperate with us, we might have to inject some unwanted drugs and carry on with our experiments. We even don't know what the reaction of such drugs on human body would be.

If you prefer to leave here alive, you have only one way that is to cooperate with us. Failing which no one in the world will know what happened to you. Few weeks from now people will forget about you and move on.

Knowing there is no other option, he agreed to their demands.

They asked him to perform all the exercise and meditations he teaches to the public and noted down various measurements and activities in his spine and brain. Especially they could see through the imaging facilities how are these ions created upon breathing are moving to his brain and get stabilized.

Following these concepts, they came out with a better ion trapping system in a membrane like living tissue which looked exactly similar to how these ions get stabilized in the brain tissues.

Alan asked mom, "I think we got what we wanted out of him. What shall we do with him?"

MOM replied," He is a guru, he had done some exercises based on what we asked. What we got out this could be a basic model"

Being a Guru, he will have his own secrets which he hasn't demonstrated before public. Just keep monitoring him. We might be able to take our research to next level with him.

"But if we keep him exposed to radiations for imaging, we might lose him.", Alan answered worriedly.

Do you have a better idea, Alan? We have to answer our investors. They have taken a big risk for us after all these years. Just work for what we need. Don't worry about him.

On top of it, more his body experience the pressure he might perform more activities to save himself from this. Monitoring him and knowing them could help take our research to next levels. Anyways he is not going to leave from here alive. Then why are you worried about him.

Time has come for us to rule this world.

By the way, to complete this research, we hired a person, do you remember him? Seems he has a breakthrough in his algorithm development. He wanted to use this quantum computer to test the concepts he had developed. I have asked him to come any time.

Smart chap, he will be here tomorrow. Please work with him and get the needed. He is the one who could complete what R.V. left. Just handle him carefully.

I am leaving now to update the investors on our research progress.

Fight...Fight...Fight...

With the help of the truck driver me and my father reached New York. When I was thinking where to go, I saw Mythili's car key in my pocket. I noticed It also had her home key. I took my father there to get refreshed before going to FBI's office.

Both of us got refreshed and met in the living room. I took my phone to call Asha to tell we are on our way to meet her. While I was about to dial her number, my father called me.

He showed me the photograph hung on the wall and asked where we are.

I told him we are in Bharath's house right now. Bharath is none other than your son in law. The person next to him in the photo is your daughter and the baby is your Grandson. He took the photo with him and sat on the couch.

After thinking for a while, he asked me where is Bharath now?

I remembered what my Sister told, that Bharath is also in New York to finish some work.

Since he was not around, I asked myself whether he might have gone to Quantum labs?

My father asked, "Where is that Quantum labs?"

I responded saying it is the same Research Labs you have worked. Seems they have renamed it.

He felt something strange and asked me to take him there.

I asked him why?

Last two days we have been debating about an algorithm to effectively give commands to Quantum computer and get answers from the measurements done on them. When he left, he mentioned he will test those concepts and come back to me.

On hearing this we both knew Bharath is really in a deep trouble.

I felt the missing case of Sadananda Guru and the algorithm Bharath is going to execute is connected in some way.

My father told twenty-five years back, they were planning to take advantage of the algorithm I wrote to their evil schemes. They killed more than eighteen spiritual leaders in an attempt to create some version of quantum computer. But they were not successful then in developing a stable version of that computer. Infact those were the evidence I collected against them that you found in the floppy disk. If they managed to develop a new computer, no doubt they were trying to reproduce their research once again.

We must go there immediately and save Bharath before he gets himself in to a big trouble.

I left a message to Mythili about my where abouts and we hired a car and proceeded to Quantum labs to stop Bharath from doing whatever he has planned.

On the way I was totally thinking about How to get out of this mess. First my Father, then me, now Bharath.

I asked my father, is there reason why you are helping Bharath knowing this research is leading to evil outcomes. You had told me you lost your life due to this, then why, why are you repeating this?

He thought for a second and answered, those are the days where technology was controlled by very few giants. If someone crack something and create something useful they wanted to make money out of it. If I had not entered Alan's lab those people would have used this quantum invention for their personal benefits, be it in ethical ways or not. Whereas today's world is connected through internet. If some one tries to use it for destructive purpose, we can come out of a way to destruct them with the same technology. If this technology doesn't reach mankind, it might take several decades before it could be created once again, by then we will lose our battle against climate change, financial crimes, Bio wars etc., That is why I agreed myself to mentor him when he came to me with questions on these topics. Even if I haven't shared my views Bharath would have found answers to that few years from now. He is a smart guy.

Once we reached the Quantum Labs, the security guard asked us the purpose of our visit. I told him I am Dinesh; we both are here to meet Mr. Singh in the cafeteria. He called and checked with him and asked us to proceed to the visitors parking and go to cafeteria to meet him.

I parked the car and went inside the cafeteria without letting anyone notice us. We saw Mr. Singh is in Storeroom checking the stock. We both went to the storeroom. On seeing us Mr. Singh was very happy and shouted Array R.V. come, come, come, how are you my friend. I know you were alive, and I will meet you some day. He hugged my father with happy tears.

I briefly informed Mr. Singh about the purpose of our visit and asked him to help us by sending a message to Bharath showing his photo.

But Mr. Singh replied, it is not like those olden days R.V. Those days we were allowed inside the building to deliver the coffee or food to employees table. After you left, they changed policy to restrict the people entering the main building. Employees now must visit cafeteria if they need something to drink or eat. But if they order online, they allow the delivery boys up till reception. You better do one thing, take this box, and pretend you want to deliver it to Bharath and try to meet him.

When I was about to take the box, my father intervened and said D, I will do this. I know this place very well.

He took the Box from me and walked towards the main building. He informed Bharath's name and said he has got a delivery. The front office staff checked and told there was no one by that name. He got alerted and asked her to check in guest list. She saw the name and tried reaching Bharath on his registered phone number. Since he didn't answer the phone, she asked him to leave the box to the security guard who would deliver it to him. After saying this she got busy responding to calls.

He then handed over the box to the guard and asked him where the rest room is. The security guard showed him the way and went inside a small room to keep the box. When he went inside, my father saw an employee entering through the door, he tailgated him and went inside the building. As he was wearing a hooded jacket to keep him warm on the snowy day, seems no one noticed him.

He kept searching for Bharath and on the way he noticed the room which he used to work. He entered the room. It seemed someone had cleaned the room and assembled new computers. There were new curtains hanging over the windows. Some one knocked the door and entered the room. My father was shocked at first. Seems it was the facilities team guy who is preparing the room for the new joiner. He looked at my father and asked him are you the new guy coming to this room? My father shook his head as if yes. That guy left a sticker on the door and asked to contact him if he has any other facility requirements.

My father saw an old carton box lying next to the cupboard. It was his belongings; he saw his family photo at the top and took it in his hands and submerged into his thoughts. Someone knocked the door once again and came in. Another shock to my father, but It was the same facilities guy once again. He said I am here to remove the carton box which I forgot to clear and took it with him.

Minutes later my father heard a familiar voice approaching the room, they stood outside the room and conversing, "You have really done a good job".

My father went inside the cupboard and hid him.

Bharath and MOM entered the room. She removed the screen from a window and showed him the Quantum computer he is going to use. It looked gigantic with probes all around and maintained in a subzero temperature.

She went on and told, you can give instructions to the computer from your table here. We have done necessary settings on your laptop.

While I was waiting to get a minute to speak to Bharath, someone else knocked the door and entered the room. It was none other than the evil scientist Alan.

Soon he entered the room, he asked Bharath can we see what you have for us?

Bharath went and connected his laptop to the quantum computer and performed small calculations. Later he tried to solve a benchmark problem in the quantum computing world. They got an answer in few minutes for the benchmark problem which would take around two hundred years in classical computer.

Everyone inside the room was amazed of this achievement. Infact that was a milestone in quantum computing arena. They congratulated Bharath on helping them achieve this quantum supremacy.

Alan was not satisfied with that. He went ahead and asked Bharath can we try to solve a little more complex problem?

Bharath replied for sure, and he spend next few minutes configuring the next problem which is little more complex than the one he had solved earlier. He went on and executed the algorithm. This time he didn't get the answers they expected.

Bharath tapped on the table and said He is right.

Who? asked MOM.

John, My mentor. Infact, he challenged me my approach would work for small set of problems only. For more complex problems it would not work as desired.

Alan interrupted him and asked then which method will work?

John won't give the answers directly. He wants us to think and bring the answers from within ourselves.

So, you mean to say there is another genius in quantum computing world other than you.

Bharath responded, "I don't know that All I can say is he is good at theoretical physics and algorithms. I don't think he had a chance to work with quantum computers before."

However, I would like to discuss with him about the results we got.

Go ahead !!! said MOM

Bharath called to John's phone immediately.

Everyone heard the ringing tone from the cupboard behind.

John disconnected the call and stepped out of the cupboard.

Everyone in the room was shocked to see him.

RV, John, RV those were the words that came out from their mouth.

Bharath asked John, what are you doing here? That too in this cupboard. How did you come here?

John looked into Bharat's eye and asked him to stop this research immediately. He warned him saying you could lose your family and your peace if you continue this research.

Bharath could not get digest what John told him. Same time the security personnel knocked the door to deliver the item he received for

Bharath. On seeing John inside the room, he shouted "He is the one delivered this for you. How did he come inside?" Then he went and locked John and asked him how he entered the building.

MOM came to senses from the shock. WoW, WoW, WoW, look at him Allan R.V. is Back.

She ordered the security to bring R.V to her office.

She also asked Bharath and Alan to join her in the office.

Since it's been more than an hour, I thought father might have gotten into some trouble. I decided to go myself inside.

I pickpocketed an ID card form the employee who came to the cafeteria. I used his ID to enter the building with other employees. I avoided the lift and went through the stairs searching for them.

When I reached the second floor, I saw an interesting lab. I saw a guy entering the room providing a pin number in the door. I noted the pin number and entered the lab few minutes later. When I went inside, I saw two person looking at computer screen monitoring something. I hid behind them and listened to them. One of them said since he is exposed to radiation for long, he might not survive for more than couple hours. One guy left the room saying, In that case I will report it to Alan.

As soon as he left, I hit the guy who stayed back and made him unconscious. I tied his hands from the behind using his Tie. When I investigated the computer screen, I see they had captured a person and monitoring him. Being a CCTV monitor I could not see the face clearly. There were some measurements and scan images being captured on the other screen.

I searched the room and found a door. I tried to open it, hit the lock with fire extinguisher, no luck. Finally, I took the ID card of the guy and scanned near the door lock. The door opened. Whom I saw inside shocked me. Yes, it was none other than Sadananda guru. I removed the probes over him and brough him out of that room. He was struggling for his life. I gave him some water to drink as he saw completely exhausted. As I removed those probes randomly there was a short-circuit and the room lost the power.

Meanwhile the second guy who went to report to Alan entered the room. Since the room was dark, he called out his colleague's name and asked is everything ok. I punched him in his nose from the front and made him fall. Then I asked where Alan is, he responded saying he is with MOM. I asked where she is. He said Sixth floor. I gave another blow on his face which made him faint.

I brough Sadananda guru out of that room and took him to the restroom. I made him seated there and informed Asha about our whereabouts to rescue us.

Then I proceeded via stairs to the sixth floor. When I opened the hallway access door from stairs slowly one of the bodyguards kept his guns on my forehead, another one asked me who are you? I fought with them and tried to advance. Hearing the noise MOM opened her office door. Seeing Bharath and Father inside the room I was careless for a fraction of a second. The bodyguards overpowered me and brought me under their control.

On seeing Bharath's reaction when I got hurt, MOM ordered her bodyguards to bring me in to her room. They cuffed my hands and left the room.

Bharath asked me, "Dinesh what are you doing here?". Then he looked at MOM and asked can you leave D. He shouted saying can anyone tell me what is going on here?

One of the bodyguard approached MOM with his tab and whispered something in her ears.

After listening to him, she looked at me and told You are that police who came searching for that Guru right?

She understood things have gone beyond her control. She warned us without demonstrating the algorithm no one is going to leave here alive.

My father knew even if we demonstrate she is not going to leave any one alive. So, he refused.

She took the gun out of her pedestal and shot in my leg.

My father cared for me and shouted stop it, I will do anything you ask, please leave them alone. That second, I felt his affection towards me.

MOM continued; Sorry RV, I will decide what is going to happen next. For now, you and Bharath carry on with the work for improving the algorithm and show us the demonstration. Otherwise, you will be the reason for this policemen death and pointed the gun on my head.

They both started working on improving the algorithm. After an hour and half, they replied we had improved the algorithm as well as the physics.

MOM ordered them to proceed with the demo.

Bharath executed the problem which failed earlier. After 12 minutes of wait they got the desired solution. Everyone in the room was astonished by this feat.

During the moment they were amazed and celebrating, I created a quick ruckus and broke Bharath's laptop into pieces.

Seeing her dream going into pieces MOM started shooting randomly with the gun in her hand. Before I overpowered the bodyguards and took control over MOM and snatched the gun from her hand, one of the bullets had scrapped Bharath's hand and another one had pierced my father's chest.

I pointed the gun over MOM, even in that situation she uttered with evil laugh no one here can go out alive. Security is very tight over here.

I asked Bharath to leave the place immediately. He was concerned about me and John. I asked him to leave the premises first and promised I would bring John out of here safely.

In the meantime, the probes I had removed in Alan's lab caused a fire and smoke raised all over the building. The fire alarms started alarming throughout the building.

Using that I created a distraction and pushed and locked MOM, Alan and guards away and carried John with me. As I climbed down the stairs, I saw two security guards approaching us with guns. I got the feeling it is going to be the end of us as we were in the gun point.

Luckily employees from the floor were running towards the door to escape the fire. Once they opened the emergency stairs door, We mingled with the crowd, hurt the guards and managed to come out of the building.

As I approached the car parking, I saw Asha and her team was already there to rescue Sadananda Guru. I made my father sit inside the car and started driving to nearest hospital. He asked me to stop the vehicle after few minutes.

My father went on saying, "I don't think I will survive this. Make me a promise. Please don't let your mother and sister know about me. They went through the grief due to my loss once, I don't want to put them in same situation once again. Please promise me".

He fainted after getting the promise. His pulse started going down. I asked him to hold on, telling him we will reach the hospital in next few minutes and will save him.

The moment we reached the hospital, my father is taken into emergency and from there taken to Operation theatre after assessing his condition. Doctors were operating him to get the bullets out and save him. Operations went on for almost three hours.

Meanwhile I was given a first aid and the bullet in my leg got removed. After 3 hours I heard a long gasp from inside the Operation theatre. Doctors came out with sad face and told me they tried hard to save him but failed. For the first time in my life my throat choked and felt a loss of some one close to me. Tears started rolling from my eyes.

My phone rang. It was my mother. Seems she felt something strange in those seconds of my father's last breath and enquired hope everything is ok with me. I hid the grief inside me and told everything is ok at my end.

My sister took the phone from my mother and asked me are you all right. Bharath called us right now. Seems you all got into a problem and fortunate enough to come out of it. I told her nothing serious, that it is a small problem, and it is all right now.

After ending the call, I saw the breaking news in the TV. Seems there was a short circuit in the one of the labs of Quantum research labs which is the cause of fire accident. Additionally, they reported there were no casualties, everyone was evacuated safely from the building. They also reported they found Sadananda Guru in that campus and rescued him in a weak and feeble condition. He is admitted to the hospital and given the required medical assistance. Detailed investigation will be conducted one he recovers completely.

With the help of Asha, I did the final rites for my father's body and returned home.

After two days I learnt from Asha, MOM and Alan were found dead mysteriously in their homes as they have been identified as suspects by Sadananda Guru in his confessions. We understood one of the investors might have done this to save their reputation.

Bharath didn't had the clue on what happened other day in the office. Sadananda Guru had no idea why he got kidnapped and what did they try to achieve using him. I and my father are the only ones who know the entire details about the case. FBI asked me and Bharath to sign a Non-Disclosure Agreement failing which we must face jail terms.

The FBI court conducted the investigations confidentially and concluded to close the case and make it classified as it involved information related to export-controlled technology that could go against nations interest if details are shared in the public. FBI had an intel on the research activities and technologies being developed at Quantum Labs and organization of similar profile from that day onwards.

Before leaving, I requested Asha to keep the details and evidence of this case as much secret especially I don't want anyone to know Bharath is involved in this case that would put him in danger, until we find those real people who are behind this crime.

Get ready for War

Two years later in Chennai, As I had disturbed sleep, I woke up from my bed and came to the hallway around 0200 AM in the morning. As I opened the window, the chilling breeze hit my face and I was mesmerized looking at the full moon. My cell phone started ringing. I picked the call and said Hello.

"Hey D, it's Asha from FBI. I got a call saying our organization intranet has been compromised. It looks like the job of well-trained team of hackers. Important thing to note is the hackers gained access to the case files we worked couple years ago and tried to steal the evidence, files, and details related to it. After copying the files, they wiped the entire directory and left a note saying, "Get Ready for War". Just take care of you and your family and try to be safe. I will share more details once I get to know more.

When I looked at the full moon once again, I saw an image of a howling wolf in it.

Murders will continue!!!

#E1.0 Rajasekar Natarajan 2022